# Flash Adopts a Puppy

## By Charlie Alexander

# Flash Adopts a Puppy

Written by Charlie Alexander
Art Work by Charlie Alexander

# At last! Today is the day to adopt a new puppy!

Flash arrives at the dog kennel.

# His name tag said "Cash".

It was because of his bright green eyes!

# Flash knew the moment he met Cash...

That the Alexander's had become a two dog family!

# Flash & Cash

Old blue eyes and new emerald green eyes...

# Becky bought Flash a new pair of green sunglasses.

They had dollar signs on them.
And they were almost as green as Cash's eyes.

Flash knew that Cash was the best puppy he could have chosen.

The Rainbow was a happy witness.

# A great day for Cash to come home!

Flash & Cash & Charlie & Becky.
Cool family!

# Flash told Cash all about his wonderful vacation.

Swimming with family is the best. Flash showed off with his famous dog paddle.

# Flash & Cash picked a whole basket of colorful flowers.

They planned to give the basket to Charlie & Becky. The cashier asked...

# "Will that be credit or Cash?"

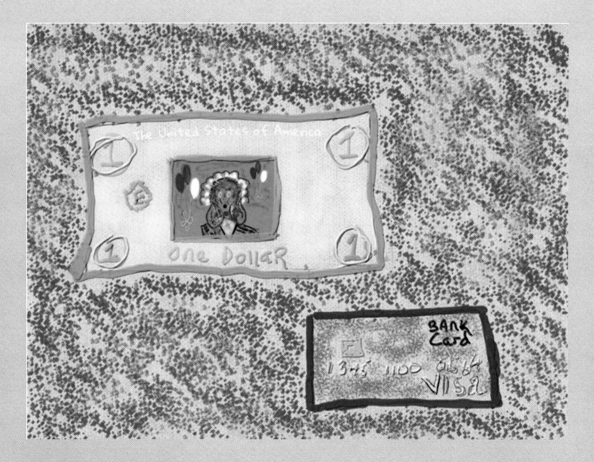

Cash hoped it would be credit!

# Everybody loves Cash!

And Flash just loves to flash "Cash"!
"Smile for the camera!"

# News flash!!

Flash may have over done taking photos!

# "I hope I don't crash" grumbled Cash!

His eyes were still blinded by Flash's flashes.

# Lunch at last!

Flash & Cash had a very big lunch!

# Now that was a lunch to dream about!

Flash & Cash were very full!

Flash was happy to show Cash where they would sleep.

But it was still too early to go to bed.

# Flash enjoyed showing Cash his own place to watch TV.

Cash felt special, welcome and happy.

# This is where our food and water is kept.

It was very clean. Charlie had swept.

# Flash showed Cash how to ask to be taken for a walk.

Cash caught on quickly

# Charlie joked "Hey Cash, don't do anything rash...

or you"ll have to clash with Flash!"

Flash & Cash had front row seats to see world renowned jazz pianist Julian Shore!

# Of course, both Cash & Flash were there for this show too...

Charlie was playing piano, Ronnie painted rhythm and Mark's voice filled the air!

# Flash & Cash made their own band. Flash tickled the keys...

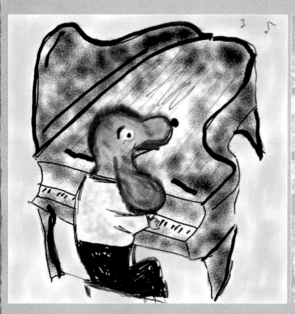 

While Cash played Bass.

# Our first Holiday ride... And Cash was already in the car.

And Flash could hardly wait any longer!

# "Everyone jumped into the car and fastened their seat belts."

One of Flash's favorite things to do...
And Cash was smiling very widely!

# It was such a good first day!

Time to go home and get ready for
bed! Well maybe not quite yet!

# Flash & Cash were filled with wonder...

So many beautiful lights!

# This year Flash's big gift was Cash!

Not money!

# Flash was looking for a gift for Cash!

Sure looks like a merry Holiday!

# Good old Flash!

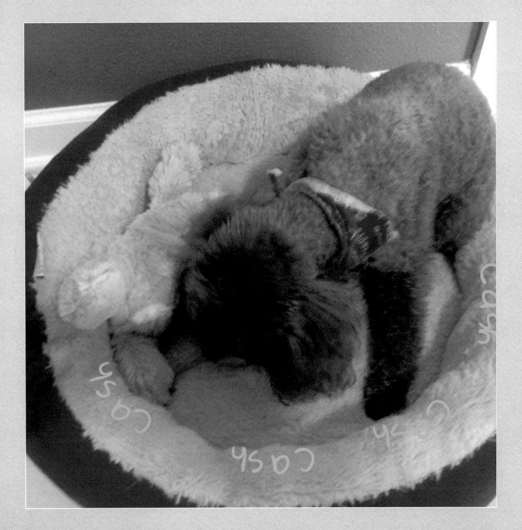

## He made a bed for Cash!

# Flash's thoughts turned to Fancy!

So now Cash was given a new job!

# It was no longer up to Flash...

To take out the trash...

# Now to remove the trash...

It simply took a little "Cash"!

# The End

Edwards Brothers Inc.
Ann Arbor MI. USA
October 18, 2017